In the Thirteenth Year

Sandra C. Satten

Alef Design Group

In the
Thirteenth
Year

Library of Congress Cataloging-in-Publication Data

Satten, Sandra C., 1960–

In the thriteenth year / Sandra C. Satten.

p.   cm.

Summary: Just before his bar mitzvah, Ike discovers that he has amazing psychic powers and that his people are from another planet, a revelation that affects his view of himself and his role in the Jewish community.

ISBN 1-881283-24-0 (alk. paper)

[1. Extrasensory perception—Fiction. 2. Extraterrestrial beings—Fiction. 3. Bar mitzvah—Fiction. 4. Jews—United States—Fiction. 5. Science fiction.] I. Title.

PZ7.S249225In   1998

[Fic]—dc21   98-22144

                                                                  CIP

                                                                  AC

ISBN# 1-881283-24-0

Published by Alef Design Group

Alef Design Group • 4423 Fruitland Avenue, Los Angeles, Ca 90058
(800) 845–0662 • (323) 582-1200 • (323) 585–0327 fax • www.alefdesign.com

manufactured in the united states of america

•1•

The Mysterious Dancing Lights

The stained glass windows gave off an eerie glow as I sat all alone in the sanctuary. I'd been in this room a hundred times before. How come I never noticed the dancing lights? I sat perfectly still watching these twelve tiny oval shaped lights bounce from floor to ceiling and wall to wall. I watched carefully trying to find out where they were coming from but they just didn't seem to come from anywhere at all. It reminded me of Starbase 12, a video game I play at the mall. The mission on Starbase 12 is to send out your twelve scout ships to find other planets that will support life. I'm usually great at video games but in Starbase 12 I can't even get past level three. That's the level where the little oval shaped ships seem to take on a life of their own. For some reason I just couldn't figure out the pattern.

The lights suddenly disappeared when Todd and his family entered the sanctuary. Todd is my best friend and today was the day he would "Become a Man." This was a joke we had since Samuel Cohen had his bar mitzvah last year. Samuel was always copying other people and his bar mitzvah speech was no exception. It sounded like he had copied his Dad's speech from 30 years ago because it started with the words, "Today I am a man." Thirty years ago practically every bar mitzvah speech started that way!

My bar mitzvah is exactly four weeks away. I thought if I came early with Todd it would help cure the stomach pains I get every time I think about standing up in front of the whole congregation and reading from the Torah. I guess concentrating on the little lights helped me feel better. Todd jumped up on the Bimah (that's the stage area) and began to goof around. "Testing one, two, three" he said from behind the little speaker stand where the Rabbi usually stood. "Today, I am a man." "Fourscore and thirteen years ago my parents brought me forth on this nation." Todd's Dad cracked a smile as he tried to be serious. "Come on Todd. Can you please behave on today of all days. This shindig is costing me a fortune and your goofing around is making your mother and me nervous." Todd saluted, military style, and answered, "Sir, yes sir." I really envied Todd. To him, this was just another day. He was as cool and calm as ever. I was probably more nervous than he was!!

●2●
Sara,
All American Girl

Shortly after Todd and his family entered the sanctuary the Saturday morning regulars began to show up. These were the families who came almost every week to Sabbath services. Mixed in were some friends and family. I knew practically all of Todd's family because we had been friends since kindergarten. As I watched the sanctuary fill up I noticed this great looking girl walk in. Something about her looked familiar but it took me a few minutes to figure out who she was. All of the sudden it hit me! Sara! It was Todd's cousin Sara! Three summers ago Sara had spent a few weeks with Todd when her parents went on a cruise. We

all had a great time. Sara was a pro at soccer and not too shabby with hoops either. She also knew some secrets to the Sonic the Groundhog video game. It was our favorite in those days.

But what happened to her! She looked terrific. As a matter of fact she looked so good I was wondering if I'd have the nerve to say hi when I saw her later. Just thinking about it made my stomach hurt.

●3●
Mazel Tov—
I Think I'm in Love

The service had started and I was following the prayer book with my eyes but my mind was totally focused on Sara. She was beautiful, like a creature from a faraway planet. (I'd been watching too much Star Trek lately.) I looked over at her and tried hard not to be obvious. Suddenly she turned her head and flashed a brilliant smile right at me. At the same time she swished her long brown hair and I heard her say, "That boy is too cute!!" ME?! Was she really looking at me when she said it? Hold on a minute, I was sitting across the aisle and at least eight rows away. I didn't even see her lips move. No way did she say that about me even if she was looking right at me. There was no way I could have heard her say anything over the loud singing of the whole congregation. "Isaac," I thought to myself, "You are really dreaming now." I made a big effort to concentrate on the rest of the service. Todd did a great job. The Torah portion he read was perfect and his speech made everybody, including Rabbi Lowenberg, laugh like crazy.

After the service we all went to the Kiddush in Todd's honor. Todd's Dad really did spend a fortune. There was ten times more food than I had ever seen at a Sabbath morning Kiddush. Todd ran over to me right after his grandfather said the prayer over the bread. "Was I great or was I great?" he said proudly. If it were anybody else I would have thought he was conceited but I knew Todd didn't really mean it that way. "Today you are a man," I answered back and the two of us slapped a high five and did our secret handshake. "Boys will be boys" I heard a voice say. You guys haven't changed that much after all. It was Sara. "Hey cuz, you look older every time I see you," Todd said. "Hey Isaac, remember my cousin Sara?" "Uh, Yeah. Uh, Hi." How stupid could I sound?! And then

Todd had to make matters worse. "What's a matter, cat got your tongue? Ike?" Sara rescued me, "Oh, he remembers me all right. I could tell by the way he looked over at me during the service." She smiled her brilliant smile again. Finally, I got up the nerve to say something. "You still shoot hoops?" Dumb, why couldn't I just relax and say something intelligent for a change. "You do remember!" Sara said triumphantly. "Isaac I still think about that summer when you guys made me an honorary member of your secret club, it was one of the best vacations I ever had." With that she reached out both hands and took one of Todd's and one of mine. We were both amazed when she performed the secret handshake, exactly as we taught her three summers ago. "Pretty good, huh?" she laughed. And by the way, cousin, you were great! Mazel Tov!

4

The Rabbi's Challenge

I took a shower around 6:30. Todd's celebration wasn't over yet. At 7:30 my parents and I were invited to a party in Todd's honor at the Manor House. At 7:30 I was looking forward to seeing Sara again. I stood in front of the mirror and combed my hair. I tried it three different ways before I finally decided on the one that looked best. I was secretly sorry that I hadn't listened to my mom about getting a haircut. "Oh, well" I said as I walked away from the mirror.

"Hey Isaac, how come Todd didn't invite me?" My little brother Shayn had just walked into the room and plopped himself down on my bed.

"Shayn, there won't be any little kids there, you'd just be bored." I lied. This was only half true. Todd is the youngest of all his cousins because his parents adopted him when they were like forty or something. So there really weren't going to be any little kids there. But I figured Shayn would have had a good time anyway, if he had been invited.

"Look at the bright side. You get to sleep over Joey's house and next month you'll definitely get to come to my party." I looked over at him to see if my brotherly advice had helped. I thought I heard him say, "Joey's dad is mean. He makes us go to bed early." But he hadn't said anything at all, he was just sitting there looking depressed.

Mom yelled from downstairs, "Shayn, get your coat on. Dad's ready to take you to Joey's."

"Bye, have fun." I said.

"Bye," he mumbled back like it was the end of the world.

Mom yelled again, "Ike, are you almost ready?"

"Yeah, Mom."

I knew we had about fifteen minutes 'til dad came back for us.

"Be down soon."

I heard the door slam when Dad and Shayn left. I knew I didn't have enough time to work on my bar mitzvah speech but I opened my bar mitzvah folder anyway. I looked over my notes on the meaning of the Bible portion I would read from the Torah on the day of my ceremony. Why did I have to get this chapter? The portion of the Torah I would read at my bar mitzvah was called Shelah Lekha. It had something to do with Moses and some spies and stuff. I knew just about everything there was to know about Moses and the Jewish people leaving Egypt. After sitting at as many Seders as I had in my lifetime I knew the whole story backwards and forwards. So why did I have to get some story I had hardly heard of before? Just to rub it in, the chapter about the spies happened almost right after the Jews got the Ten Commandments. I saw the whole movie three times and not once did I see anything about any spies.

Rabbi Lowenberg had said it didn't matter that I never heard much about it before. He said every parashah, every Bible chapter, was important in some way. And then when I wasn't expecting it, he did It. It, was the Rabbi's challenge. In a way it wasn't fair because he only made the challenge to the smart kids. Todd had told me he'd do It and right after I told him I didn't know a thing about Shelah Lekha, he did.

"You know Isaac, you can learn this. You need to have some confidence in yourself. If you study the chapter in English I bet you'll understand it enough to give your own sermon. Isaac, I sometimes give the bar mitzvah a chance to give his own thoughts on the meaning of the Torah portion. It's called a D'var Torah, a word of Torah, and it isn't very hard to do. If you agree to take the challenge, I promise I won't speak at your entire ceremony other than to conduct the service."

It wasn't fair! I already had enough to do to prepare for my Torah reading and service. How could he be asking me to prepare a D'var Torah on top of everything else? Wasn't there a law against

Rabbis who made bets with their students? I wanted to answer "No Way!" but I didn't. "I don't know Rabbi..." I began.

"Confidence, Isaacle. You need to believe in yourself and then you can accomplish anything."

"Well, I...I'll try." What was I saying? Had I lost my mind?

Now, as I read the Shela͟h Lekha chapter over in the English translation it made practically no sense at all. How was I ever going to give a D'var Torah on a story I didn't understand?! I closed the folder in time to hear my Dad honk the horn.

❧5❧
Broken Glasses

On the way to the Manor I started rehearsing ways to ask Sara to dance. I didn't want to sound stupid like this morning. Should I ask her for a fast dance or a slow dance? I decided that it would be best to start off fast and see how it went from there. When we pulled up, I saw Sara going in the front door with her parents. My stomach began to feel a little funny.

"Todd's little cousin Sara really grew up since that summer she visited." Mom said.

"Yeah." I answered casually trying hard not to sound too interested. As the waiters passed out weird stuff to eat I saw Todd in a corner of the room getting his picture taken. When the photographer was done I told Todd of my plan to ask Sara to dance.

"What's the big deal?" He said as he grabbed a few unrecognizable things off a passing food tray and wolfed them down.

"None, I guess. Do you think she'll say yes?" "Of course, you idiot. She's not gonna want to stand around all night without dancing."

I had to admit Todd's advice did seem to make sense. "Who you callin' an idiot, you dork!" I gave him a shove when I said it and the next thing I knew I heard Sara's voice right behind me.

"Are you guys at it, again?"

I was hoping she hadn't heard our whole conversation.

"Hey Sara, Isaac wants to know if you'll dance with him later." I could have killed him right then and there. Thankfully it didn't take Sara long to answer, "Sure, um, definitely." This time Todd had caught her off guard. She looked as embarrassed as I felt. I hoped she didn't think I was too wimpy to ask her myself. Trying to recover some dignity, I rolled my eyes at Todd and added "I was going to ask you myself until Mr. Matchmaker here butted in."

Sara laughed. "I guess we'll just have to take it from here."

That whole night was great. Sara and I danced five times together. The last time I finally got up the nerve to ask her to slow dance. In between she helped me learn some new line dances. Oh, and during one of the Hora dances I got to help pick Todd up on a chair and dance him around. Even six feet up in the air Todd looked cool as can be. His mother though looked like she was about to faint. Especially when we accidentally tipped the chair and Todd's glasses went flying off into the middle of the dance floor. Except for Todd's broken glasses, it was a great weekend. So great, in fact, I was actually looking forward to my own bar mitzvah celebration.

●6●
The Sisters Susan

Todd called me up at noon on Sunday. He sounded like he was half-asleep. "You wanna go to the mall" he mumbled. "You just wake-up?" I asked. "Uh huh" he mumbled again. "Mom wants to get my glasses fixed." When we got to the mall Todd and his mom went straight to Eyewear Central. "I'll meet you at the arcade in an hour," I said, as I took the opportunity to cut out on my own. Since I had an hour to kill I figured I'd stop by the card store to see if I could find a nice card to send Sara. I didn't get too far when I got distracted by the Sisters Susan. They are this idiotic trio of girls at my school who call each other Susan and sister all the time. The weird thing is, they're not sisters and not one of them is really named Susan. Anyway, having some time to kill and knowing these girls had a bad reputation, I followed them into the drug store. They looked so guilty I knew they were up to no good. Sure enough, Susan and Susan went into the make up aisle and the other Susan walked up to the cashier and started coughing her head off. "Do you have any cough drops?" she choked out between her fake coughs. Everybody in the store was looking at her because she acted like she was choking to death or something. As the cashier came out from behind the counter to help her grab some cough drops, I noticed the other two Susans slipping nail polish into their knapsacks. "I knew it, I knew it." I said to myself. "I wish I could grab the stuff and put it back just to see the look on their faces when they can't find it!" To my absolute amazement, just after I thought it, the two Susans got to the end of the aisle and I noticed the nail polish, one pink and one red, fly right out of their sacs and down the aisle. They landed perfectly right back in the display case where they were taken from. Before I could even think about what I had

just seen, the manager came running from the back of the store yelling, "Don't let those girls leave!" The cashier ran over and politely asked the girls to wait. At the same time, two mall security guards arrived and one of the Susans looked like she was about to cry. The coughing one looked sort of nervous as she tried her best to blend in with the crowd of people watching. "What's your problem?" said the third Susan as she narrowed her eyes at the manager. "Ever hear of shoplifting?" He said back. "Shop what? " she said in a mock tone as if she either didn't hear him or didn't understand English.

I followed the manager, the security guards, and the two Susans as they headed toward the mall office. The third Susan (the coughing one) slunk along behind me all the way.

"Hey, Segal! What are you doin' hangin' out here?" She pulled me closer and said, "If you think you saw anything I know you're brainy enough not to be a snitch!"

"I didn't see anything except you coughing and making a giant fool out of yourself. I'm hangin' out because this was just too good to miss!! Besides, it's a free country."

Five minutes later the security office door opened up and the girls came walking out. They looked sort of dazed , but as soon as they were clear of the office, they broke into wide grins and told Sherry (the coughing Susan) what had happened.

"Sherry, you won't believe it! They made us dump out everything in our sacs and the nail polishes weren't there. They just plain vanished! "Sherry looked at them disapprovingly like they had just failed a big test. "I knew you guys were chicken!!"

The two Susans looked at each other and started to insist that they weren't chicken and that they really had taken the nail polish. But Sherry walked away from them mumbling how she had done her part and made a fool of herself choking in public and that they were just a couple of chickens.

The whole thing was so funny that I couldn't wait to tell Todd. And then it occurred to me that I had caused it! Yeah...I had wished I could put back the nail polish, and then, they floated right out of the girls backpacks and onto the shelf. What was I supposed to tell Todd? This was crazy!! I decided to keep my mouth shut, at least for now.

●7●
Just too Weird

I was thinking about Sara as I got off the bus on Monday. I was thinking about her in Math class and History and even gym that I am usually totally involved in. The only other thing I really thought about that whole day was the "Sisters Susan" incident at the mall. I saw one of the Susans in the hall between classes. Rumor had it that they had a big fight and they weren't sisters anymore. As a matter of fact they were back to using their real names Sherry, Daphne, and Laura. The "Sisters Susan" were no more and I figured that society was probably a lot better off.

When I got home after school I asked my mom if I could invite Sara to my bar mitzvah. The invitations had already been sent out and I already invited two more friends than mom said I could but I thought it was worth a shot.

"Pleee...ase, Mom. I really like her. I don't even know if she can come." I used my best begging voice and hoped that my mother wouldn't say no to just one more person.

Mom pulled out an extra invitation.

"Sure, honey." I thought I heard her say. Suddenly I realized that her lips hadn't moved. She handed me the invitation.

"Sure, honey" she said.

My stomach began to feel strange. I smiled a weak thank you and bolted, like lightning, upstairs to my room. Mom must have thought I was excited about the invitation but really I was worried about what was happening to me. Am I going crazy? I thought to myself as I flung the invitation towards my desk. It ricocheted off my computer screen and landed on my desk chair. "I can't even make a simple shot to my desk anymore!" As soon as I said it the bar mitzvah invitation floated up off the chair and landed on my keyboard. It was standing straight up between the keys!! This is too weird! Just too weird.

•8•
Nightmare on the Bimah

That night I woke up in a cold sweat. I dreamed I was standing on the bimah at my bar mitzvah. I had finished reading the Torah portion and had begun to give my speech. I opened my mouth to start and the only thing that I could say was AROPSAID NAM-A-MA, AROPSAID NAM-A-MA. People were looking at me like I was from a strange planet or something and my little brother Shayn was mimicking and making fun of me. "AROPSAID NAM-A-MA, AROPSAID NAM-A-MA."

Then the whole congregation including the Rabbi, my parents, and Sara were chanting

AROPSAID NAM-A-MA, AROPSAID NAM-A-MA, louder and louder and louder until I just couldn't stand it anymore! STOP!! STOP!!

I woke myself up yelling at them to stop. I couldn't go back to sleep that whole night. The words AROPSAID NAM-A-MA, AROPSAID NAM-A-MA just kept swimming in my brain, over and over and over. I was afraid to close my eyes. I didn't want to fall asleep and have the dream again. Somehow, I knew that if I closed my eyes, the dream would return.

❦9❦
AROPSAID NAM-A-MA

Wednesday morning I must have looked terrible 'cause I didn't even have to convince mom that I was sick and needed to stay home from school. Nothing was really wrong with me other than I was exhausted from lack of sleep, scared to death that I was losing my mind, and afraid that I was turning into some kind of freak. Mom tried to make me feel better. She brought me tea and reminded me that my bar mitzvah was still three weeks away.

"Your friend Todd survived it and you will too." Then she added, "Stop worrying so much, you'll be fine! I've got to get Shayn ready for school. Dad's already having breakfast so come down soon if you're hungry. "I didn't say anything and purposely let mom think she knew what the trouble was. Just then I heard my bus go by outside. At least I got to skip a day of school.

I sipped the tea and tried to decide if it was worth getting out of bed just to eat breakfast. I wasn't that hungry but I was still nervous about closing my eyes and falling asleep again. I pulled myself out of bed and headed downstairs.

By the time I got down mom was kissing Shayn and sending him out the door to his bus. I melted into the chair and stared into my cereal bowl. In my head or maybe Dad's head I heard him reading the weather in the newspaper. "Gonna be a nice day." he said. "Why so gloomy, Ikey?" I couldn't hold back anymore, I had to tell him.

"AROPSAID NAM-A-MA" was the only thing I seemed to be able to blurt out.

"Whoa, wait a minute," I heard him think. "Sandy! Sandy!" he called my mother. "Come here quick!"

Mom ran into the kitchen. She took a look at my Father's face and then at me. Dad's face was an ear to ear grin.

"AROPSAID NAM-AM-A?" mom asked excitedly?

"AROPSAID NAM-AM-A." Dad echoed back as if to confirm her question.

•10•
The Family Secret

"Will somebody please tell me what on earth is going on here?" Dad laughed, "It has nothing to do with earth!" It was very strange. Neither one of them had moved their lips and yet I knew exactly what they were thinking! "Nothing to do with earth?" I repeated, but I still didn't get it. Mom began first, "You see honey, it all began a long time ago. Back when the Jews were wandering in the desert for forty years, small groups of Jews broke off and settled in different places along the way. Our tribe was able to survive because of a very smart man called HAON. HAON was a man of science and was always inventing tools that allowed us to live in places no one else could. One night he had a

dream in which God told him to build a space ark. Like Noah, HAON spent many years of his life designing and building a great space ship. When the ship was complete HAON's family and many of our tribal members were convinced that they were chosen to go. They left the Earth and were guided to a planet whose ecosystem was close enough to Earth for our colony to survive and grow!

A few years later the planet was named AROPSAID that is backwards for the Diaspora.

"Diaspora? Isn't that what happened to the Jewish people after the Temple was destroyed and there wasn't any place to gather in prayer?"

"Yes Isaac, the Jewish people are still in Diaspora. That's why we say "Next year in Jerusalem" hoping that HA'ISSEM, I mean Messiah will come and unite the Jewish people again. When we left AROPSAID there was hope that the HA'ISSEM (that's backwards for Messiah) would someday unite us on our home planet." The whole story was incredible and I felt myself wanting to know more.

"How come you and Daddy left AROPSAID? And what does all this have to do with me being able to read minds and move things around just by thinking about it? And what in the universe is AROPSAID NAM-A-MA?"

●11●
In the 13th Year

Dad took over the story. "You see Isaac, about twenty-five years ago a terrible disease called SACHS-TAY broke out on AROPSAID and many people died. It was a sad moment in AROPSAID history when we realized that the only way to save our people was to leave AROPSAID behind. Twelve scout ships were sent throughout the galaxy and when they returned a few hundred thousand of our people left with each scout. In our case we returned to earth knowing that there were many places we could live and still be free to practice our Judaism.

"But what is AROPSAID NAM-AM-A?" I repeated knowing that I was finally close to understanding the secret.

Mom broke in again, "The first few years were difficult here on Earth. We had to learn about Jewish life here and also adjust to the way our bodies worked."

"You mean this isn't really what my body looks like?!" My mind started racing through all the episodes of Star Trek remembering all the different aliens I'd ever seen. I began to wonder which one of them I looked like the most in my true AROPSAIDian form. I was interrupted by Dad who was laughing like crazy. His laughing was beginning to bug me.

"Isaac, We're not inhabiting different bodies. Our bodies just work differently here on earth. On AROPSAID when a boy's body and mind begin to mature at the same rate he is experiencing NAM-A-MA. For a girl it's called NAMOW-A-MA. It happens somewhere around age 12 or 13, usually in the 13th year of the child's life. Here on earth we experience two of the powers we developed while living on AROPSAID. The ability to read minds and levitate objects. On AROPSAID the powers last forever once you mature but on Earth they only last a short time each year.

"How long dad, how long will my powers last?" I was beginning to think this could be a lot of fun now that I knew I wasn't losing my mind anymore.

"Dad thought a moment, it was so cool how he didn't even have to speak and I could hear him actually thinking. "For girls, the powers last around two to three months. Of course, pregnant woman and nursing mothers have the powers all the time."

"Wow!" I suddenly had a flashback to the year my brother was born. I was only six at the time but I remember watching my mother float a diaper across the room. She looked so embarrassed when she realized I saw her that I never mentioned it again. As a matter of fact, this was the first time I'd even thought about it since then.

And then there were a few times when Dad seemed to know all the details of something I had tried so hard to hide. Like the time Todd and I had ridden our bikes to the next town where they had just opened this new comic book store. We were ten at the time and the only way to get there was to ride our bikes for about two miles along interstate 9. Dad was furious the minute I walked in the door and said something about a neighbor who had called and told him we were out on the highway. It was hard to believe anyone had recognized us because we had purposely tied our sweat jacket hoods real tight around our faces. Dad also seemed to know a lot of the details that happened to us that day. I remember thinking that it was almost as if he had read my mind!

"Dad, so how long will my powers last?"

"Well, mine usually last about 30 days."

"Thirty days! Rip off!!" I said out loud. "That's hardly enough time to get used to them."

"Whoa! Slow down," said Dad. "You have to be very careful with your powers Isaac. I'm not telling you not to use them but part of becoming a man is to understand the importance of keeping our secret. You mustn't tell anyone, not even Todd. And watch out with the mind reading. Sometimes it's better not to know someone that well!"

"It can also be a great distraction, Isaac," Mom warned; "So please just be careful."

•12•
Isaac Segal,
Alien Lunatic

Things were almost normal by Thursday. If you could call being telepathic and having levitation powers normal. Actually, now that I understood that I was an Aropsaid it wasn't unusual at all. As a matter of fact, it was turning out to be a lot of fun. Take Thursday morning for example, when my dog Shalom came in for breakfast I moved his bowl a few inches just as he was about to drink. I tried to read his mind to see what he was thinking when it happened but I couldn't pick up any signals. I guess dogs are on a different wavelength or something.

Todd and I rode our bikes to school. We talked about video games practically the whole way. On Sunday, at the arcade, I had finally beaten the third level of Starbase 12. In fact, the whole game seemed so easy that I would have beaten it except I ran out of tokens on the last level. The weird thing was that Todd couldn't beat level three even though he spent about five dollars trying. He just couldn't track the movement of the scout ships. I finally dragged him away to a new game I found called Robotic Alien Lunatics.

All the way to school I was tempted to tell Todd about my powers. I didn't because somewhere in my brain I imagined him nicknaming me "the Alien Lunatic."

Besides it would be just too difficult to explain and I knew I had to keep the secret. "AROPSAID NAM-A-MA," I said to myself and I couldn't have been prouder than if I'd just beaten the hardest video game on Earth. "AROPSAID NAM-A-MA" It was funny how since I started Hebrew school I'd been looking forward to my bar mitzvah and being recognized as a grown-up. Every celebration of every friend including Todd was special. Being able to slip on a tallit and read the Torah in front of the entire congregation really meant something. Suddenly, I found myself wondering if the moment would still be special for me, too, or if being an AROPSAID would make my bar mitzvah less important. Knowing I was AROPSAID sure wasn't helping me write my speech any faster.

"He-llo-o-o. Anybody home?" I heard Todd humming the Twilight Zone theme song in his head, the other stuff he was saying aloud trying to get my attention.

"Earth to Segal." "I read you loud and clear." I answered. I must have been fiddling with the combination to my locker for at least ten minutes. Every time I made eye contact with someone I realized I could read their thoughts. It was mind boggling!

On the way to Math I passed one of the old Sisters Susan. It was Sherry, the coughing sister.

"Isaac Segal is pretty cute. I wonder if he likes anybody?" Ugh! Why did I have to hear that?

"Sara," I tried to think back. "I really like Sara." Maybe the telepathy worked both ways and if I thought hard enough I could pass her the message. I don't think it worked because she gave me this wide toothy smile as I passed by. From now on, I'll definitely have to be more careful whose thoughts I read.

•13•
Grasshoppers and Punishment

Thursday, after school I met with Rabbi Lowenberg to prepare for my Torah portion and to make sure I could lead all the prayers for the Friday night services. The service part was easy. I'd been coming to Friday night services with my family for years. I could recite every prayer without even looking at the prayer book. The Torah portion was a little harder. Just knowing that all eyes and ears would be focused on me during the reading was enough to make me sick. I wished I could just get up and joke around the way Todd did. To him, none of this was a big deal. At least on Saturday I wouldn't have to lead too much of the service. The Rabbi usually did most of that.

The Rabbi was on the phone when I arrived so I waited quietly in the study next to his office. I still hadn't written my speech and thought maybe I could get an idea if I read over the Torah portion in English again. I did remember one thing I heard about the spy story. One of my Hebrew teachers once told us that the Jews wandered forty years in the desert as a punishment for not believing the two spies who reported that they could take over the land of Canaan. Each of the twelve tribes sent a representative to spy on Canaan and to see if they could take over the land by force. When they came back only two of the spies believed that Canaan could be conquered, the other ten said "no way." My teacher said that most of the tribes were so used to being slaves that they didn't believe they had any power to fight. It even says they were afraid of getting stepped on like grasshoppers. God told Moses that since the majority of the people had no faith, their punishment would be to wander in the desert for forty years. One year, for each day the

Spies were away in Canaan. Weird. If the slaves were made to wander in the desert forty years as a punishment for not believing some spies, it made me wonder how long AROPSAIDians would wander around on the earth and if maybe it was some sort of punishment.

Rabbi Lowenberg had just come in the room when the strangest thing happened. He looked right into my eyes and thought, "None of us knows for sure, Isaacle, we can only wait and hope that HA'ISSEM will come and gather all of us AROPSAID and send us home." It took me a few minutes to figure out that the Rabbi must have read my mind. It seemed crazy but I tried communicating with him telepathically. "Rabbi," I thought, "You are one of us?"

"Yes," he said. "My whole family died during the SACHS-TAY plague on AROPSAID. I survived but I miss my birthplace and all that was once familiar."

"I'm sorry," I answered aloud. "Now that I'm a NAM-A-MA I understand how difficult life can be."

I noticed the Rabbi brush away what looked like a tear. He cleared his voice and then pointed to the Hebrew page in front of me. "Come Isaacle, you may be NAM-A-MA but you have only three weeks to prepare for your bar mitzvah. Your NAM-A-MA powers will come and go but your Judaism will be with you always. There is still much work for you to prepare and I'm also expecting a D'var Torah as good as my own sermon."

Nothing like a little Rabbi pressure to upset the stomach. Now, I wasn't only worried about my speech but I had to be extra careful not to let my mind wander during our study sessions!

•14•
Sara's Coming!

On Friday night Todd and I went to services together. We got to be ushers, greeting everyone good Sabbath and handing out the prayer books as people came in. Later, during the service, the Rabbi gave Todd the honor of saying the prayer over the wine because he was the most recent bar mitzvah. At the end of the service I was invited up to lead the Adon Olam. After the service as the Rabbi shook my hand I heard him think, "You're ready, Isaacle. You'll do a great job. Only two more weeks." I shook his hand. "Good Sabbath Rabbi," I said as I tried hard not to think about the bar mitzvah speech I still hadn't written. Bad move, the Rabbi must have been tuned in to my thoughts because he added. "Isaac, review the list I told you to write at our first lesson and read the Torah portion over in English a few more times. I know you'll be able to come up with something interesting; after all, you have always been our top student in Hebrew School." I thought about it and knew he was right. One year, back in third grade, I had even been voted most Rabbinical. At the time, I didn't even know what it meant until my Dad explained that it meant I asked a lot of good questions. Looking at the list might help. It was an assignment the Rabbi gave to everyone at their very first lesson in preparation for bar mitzvah. He had asked me to make a list of things I was thankful for, things I looked forward to, and things I wanted to do someday. I wrote a few ideas down but they didn't have anything to do with my Torah portion. Maybe I'd have better luck if I took the Rabbi's advice and read the chapter in English a few more times. The whole thing was making me nervous. I was beginning to wish I'd never accepted the Rabbi's Challenge.

I found Todd in the next room where the kiddush was being served. He was stuffing his mouth with a brownie when he mumbled something about Sara. I didn't really understand him with his mouth full but I read his mind so I knew exactly what he was trying to say.

"Todd!! I can't believe you didn't tell me!" It seemed that Todd forgot to mention that Sara's mom had called his mom and said that Sara could come to my bar mitzvah. They lived four hours away by car but she could send Sara by train if Todd's parents would pick her up Thursday evening at the station.

"You mean Sara's coming! Excellent!!" This was great. I guess it meant she liked me enough to go to all this trouble.

"Hey Todd, do you think she likes me?"

"Duh!" He replied. "No, I think she's coming because she just loves attending services with her favorite cousin."

As soon as he answered he shoved another brownie in his mouth. Conversation over. I knew there was no point in trying to ask him anything more so I tried reading his mind just to see if he'd forgotten to tell me anything else. "Mmmmm, great brownies. I wonder if there are anymore. I hope Mrs. Segal picks us up soon. I hate this new shirt. It's soooo itchy!" I tuned Todd out, if he had any other information about Sara it certainly wasn't the first thing on his mind.

I spotted one brownie left on a tray at the other end of the table. When no one was looking, I levitated the other cookies to cover it over. Then I strolled down to the end of the table and uncovered my buried treasure. "Where'd you find that?" I heard Todd say from behind me. "Right here." I replied. "I guess it was sort of hidden under the cookies." Todd shrugged and picked up a cookie. He was still chewing it when we went outside to wait for my mother.

•15•
Mom's Surprise

It had been three and a half weeks since Todd's bar mitzvah and the beginning of my NAM-A-MA powers. If Dad was right I'd be losing my powers any day and wouldn't have them again for a whole year! I hoped they would at least last long enough for me to see Sara. It wasn't really nice, but I was planning to read her mind so I would know for sure if she liked me as much as I liked her.

Sara would be coming in on Thursday after school. I was thrilled. It meant that if I could slip away from all my visiting relatives for a while I could see her an extra time before my bar mitzvah. Thursday took forever to arrive and when it did it was the longest day of my entire life. At lunchtime I skipped lunch and went to the library to work on my speech. I picked up my pen but got nowhere because all I could think about was Sara. When the bell rang and I realized I hadn't written one solitary word I panicked. All through the afternoon my stomach was tied up in knots. I don't really know what that means but for some reason I pictured a piece of red string licorice tied up so tight that you couldn't even bite it if you wanted to.

When I got home from school I went straight up to my room and promised myself I wouldn't move until I had written something–Anything. By now I was so desperate I would have considered copying Samuel Cohen's dad's speech. The thought of it cracked me up. After twenty minutes passed I couldn't take it anymore. I guess not eating lunch was getting to me. It also didn't help that mom was downstairs getting ready for company. A lot of my relatives were coming for dinner. Mom had ordered platters from the deli but she was still cooking up a storm of side dishes like potato kugel, kasha with bow ties, and my favorite, meatballs. It was the smell of the meatballs that did it. I wandered downstairs.

"Mom, I'm hungry. Can I have some meatballs?" Mom took out a plate and gave me three huge meatballs. Then I heard her thinking. "I have a surprise for you." I spoke aloud so she would know I heard her.

"Mom, Tell me the surprise. You know I hate surprises anyway!" I didn't wait for her to speak but I tried to read her mind as I ate the meatballs. I didn't get it all but I knew for sure it had something to do with Sara. Mom must have known it was hard to read minds with your mouth full because she didn't wait long to answer.

"I invited Todd, his parents, and Sara over for dinner." I stopped chewing long enough to give Mom a gigantic kiss. "Thanks Mom, you're the best!" This meant that Sara would be coming in about one hour. I finished my last meatball and practically flew upstairs to straighten my room and jump in the shower.

•16•
Not the Only AROPSAIDian on the Planet

By the time Sara and Todd arrived my house was full of relatives. It was so loud you could barely hear people talking. I tried to read Sara's mind but with so many people so close by I just kept getting bits and pieces of everybody's thoughts. None of it made any sense.

After dinner, Sara, Todd, and I went into my room to play my new CD- ROM game called Ultra Mondo Warriors. In less than five minutes Todd had taken over the game and it looked like his turn was going to last awhile. My mind started wandering as I began to think about ways I could ask Sara to go out with me.

"Sara, you know I like you and I think you like me; will you go steady with me." Nah, too seventies.

"Sara will you go out with me?"

"Of course I will Isaac. You don't have to think of any more ways to ask me. You know I will!"

I looked over at her in disbelief.

"What?! Did you say something?"I looked right at her. Her lips didn't move. "Of course I'll go out with you, Isaac."

I stared at her in amazement. This isn't happening. "Can you read my thoughts?"

Sara answered, "Either that or you must be dreaming."

"How is this happening?" I asked.

"You're not the only AROPSAIDian on the planet, you know!"

"I know, but what about Todd? Does he know? At that moment Todd's turn ended and he broke in.

"Hey, you two look like a couple of lovebirds. Sittin' there on the bed and just staring at each other without talking. If this is gonna get personal, let me know and I'm outta here!"

Sara and I laughed aloud at how funny we must have looked just staring at each other and having an entire telepathic conversation. We jumped up from the bed and moved closer to the computer. I glanced at Sara, she shook her head and I heard a voice inside her head say, "No, Todd has no clue."

I looked around my room trying to buy some time so we could finish the conversation. I used my powers to turn off the switch on my computer so Todd would have to restart the game.

"Hey, what gives?" Todd mumbled. I knew I had messed up his chance at the high score.

"I guess it bombed out." I answered. "Start it up again and we'll play something else."

As soon as Todd was involved in starting the computer up again I thought to Sara, "What about Todd. Will he become NAM-A-MA too?" Just then Sara put her arm around her cousin Todd and said,

"I'm glad your mom and dad adopted you Todd. I wouldn't want anyone else fixing me up with their best friend. Isaac and I want to know if it's okay with you if we go steady?" Sara winked at me knowing she had answered all my questions at once.

"Gee, what do I care." shrugged Todd. "Just don't get all choked up and kissy kissy in front of me and you have my blessing."

I looked over at Sara. She smiled back and without saying a word I took her hand and gave it a gentle squeeze.

•17•
Waking Up to Reality

Friday morning I woke up around 5 a.m.. It was way too early to get out of bed so I just lay there staring up at the ceiling. The night before kept playing in my mind like an instant replay caught on videotape.

Sara was an AROPSAID and she was NAMOW-A-MA at the same time I had my NAM-A-MA powers. It was too fantastic to believe. I felt like it was all something out of a science fiction movie.

I looked over at my alarm and knew it would be going off soon. It was set for 5:30 because I still had to write my speech. I was angry with myself for not writing it before now. It wasn't just the chapter about the spies that made it so hard to write. It was the feeling that I'd had ever since I found out about AROPSAID NAM-A-MA and my new powers. Nothing sounded as important as AROPSAID NAM-A-MA. To say in my speech that becoming a bar mitzvah was a turning point in my life wasn't even true anymore. How could becoming a Jewish adult measure up to becoming an alien with super powers?

As the clock turned to 5:29 I knew I'd run out of time. I only had an hour and a half before I had to get ready for school. When the alarm went off I focused my energy and thought hard to turn it off. This was a trick I'd been doing for a few weeks already.

"Buzzzzzz...zzzz...zzzzzz." Nothing happened.

I closed my eyes and concentrated harder. Still nothing.

"Come on, Isaac," I coached myself. "Think harder."

It was no use. I knew exactly what was happening to me. Just to be sure I tried something different.

"Door open," I said aloud. "Open!!!" I yelled louder.

Nothing! I didn't want to believe it; I tried hard not to cry as I felt a tear rolling down my cheek. My NAM-A-MA powers were gone!

•18•
M-A-MA I, YADOT

I smashed the alarm button with my fist as I got out of bed to look at the calendar on my desk. I counted out the days since Todd's bar mitzvah. Twenty eight, twenty-nine, thirty. Thirty days, exactly thirty days. I sat there staring at myself in the mirror on the back of my door. I looked like the same Isaac Segal on the outside but I felt totally empty on the inside.

Without my powers, I was just plain old Isaac Segal, regular ordinary kid. Boring! I glanced at the corkboard on the back of my desk and noticed the list I had started so many months ago. It seemed like my first bar mitzvah lesson with the Rabbi was so long ago. I was a Whole different person since I wrote that list. Out of curiosity, I picked up the list and looked at it. There were three columns. 1) Things I am thankful for, 2) Things I look forward to, and 3) Things I want to do in my life.

The thankful list included...

a) great parents who love me

b) A little brother who looks up to me and makes me feel ten feet tall when I'm only five.

c) Todd, my best friend who truly understands my love of video games, Star Trek, and comic books.

I picked up a pen and added a fourth thing.

d) Sara, a girlfriend who shares my secret.

I looked at the next column; Things I look forward to...

a) driving a car

b) going to college

c) becoming a bar mitzvah, wearing a tallit, reading from the Torah, and celebrating the day with all my friends and family.

Things I want to do in my life...

a) Take a trip to Israel

b) Be a computer software designer and design virtual reality games.

c) Buy a sports car or an antique car and fix it up myself. I picked up the pen and wrote...

d) Visit the planet AROPSAID

As I looked over the list, not much had changed since I first wrote it. I was the same person I was four months ago when I began my bar mitzvah lessons. For the first time since becoming NAM-A-MA and finding out I was an alien, my life made sense. I was me, Isaac Segal, regular Jewish kid. My powers had opened up a new part of me but it was still a Jewish part. The powers were gone but I was still the same Jewish kid as always who was about to be magically transformed into a Jewish Adult. I was still looking forward to my bar mitzvah, to reading from the Torah, and even going to Israel someday.

I took out a clean piece of paper and began to write. The words flew out of my pen faster than I could write them down. When I got to the last paragraph I wrote...

...The majority of the Jews who left Egypt still thought like slaves. They didn't believe in themselves; they had no faith that they could win over the land of Canaan even though they had just witnessed great miracles upon leaving Egypt. They somehow forgot that God was on their side.

We have been in the Diaspora for almost two thousand years. It would be easy for us to forget our faith, to forget that God is on our side, but we can't. We must believe that Messiah will come and we will all be, "Next year in Jerusalem!" and let us say "Amen."

I looked up to see myself grinning in the mirror.

"Not bad, Segal," I announced to myself. "Not bad at all."

The next morning as I waited for my parents and Rabbi Lowenberg in the sanctuary I saw the lights again. The twelve dancing lights were shining through the stained glass windows right by the picture of the Twelve Tribes. This time, I could tell where the lights were coming from and I knew exactly where they were going. I jumped up on the bimah, looked out at the empty seats, and declared...

"NAM-A-MA I, YADOT."

Translation: "TODAY, I AM A MAN."

Middle Readers and Young Adult Titles from Alef Design Group

Bar Mitzvah Lessons

Martin Elsant

David Silverberg is the worst bar mitzvah student in all of recorded Jewish history. No one can teach him until his father takes him to Rabbi Reuven Weiss, a mechanic and a rebel. This novel is the story of how they change each other's lives and how David grows to become a bar mitzvah.

ISBN #1-883123-01-1. Ages 11-13. Softcover. $5.95

Champion & Jewboy

Bruce M. Siegel

Champion & Jewboy are two novellas dealing with anti-Semitism. In *Champion*, a sixteen-year-old digs into his grandfather's hidden past. *Jewboy* features a teenager convicted of vandalizing a synagogue who is transported back through time to witness, and become a participant in, a number of the most famous anti-Semitic events of the twentieth century.

ISBN #1-883123-11-9. Ages 10-14. Softcover. $6.95

Dear Hope...Love, Grandma

Hilda A. Hurwitz and Hope R. Wasburn
Edited by Mara H. Wasburn

When eight-year-old Hope is assigned the school project of corresponding with a senior citizen, her grandmother, Hilda, proceeds to unfold the stories of her childhood in turn-of-the-century St. Louis.

ISBN #1-883123-03-8. Ages 8-11. Hardcover. $13.95

New! Gabriel's Ark

Sandra R. Curtis

This story lesson is about a family that helps a fearful boy with special needs through his bar mitzvah experience. It opens up the question of inclusion and dealing with disabilities.

ISBN # 1-881283-23-2. Ages 8-11. Softcover. $5.95

The Grey Striped Shirt

Jacqueline Jules

A critically-acclaimed middle reader chapter book, _The Grey Striped Shirt_ gently introduces students to the Holocaust through the eyes of Frannie, a young girl who discovers her grandmother's concentration camp uniform while looking through her closet.

ISBN #1-883123-21-6. Ages 8-11. Softcover. $8.50

New! Keeping Faith in the Dust

Fran Maltz

Keeping Faith in the Dust is a unique recounting of a familiar story—the siege of Masada in the first century C.E.—from the diary of a teenage girl. This is the personal tale of Hannah who begins her journal as a young girl of thirteen while living in Ein Gedi and ends with a sixteen-year-old Hannah during the final fight on Masada.

ISBN #1-881283-25-9. Ages 10-14. Softcover. $6.95

New! Let's Talk About the Sabbath

Dorothy K. Kripke

Off the pen of a well respected Jewish children's author, Let's Talk About the Sabbath is a young person's guide to the Sabbath. From meeting the Queen of the Sabbath, to celebrating Havdallah, this book delights in the visions of a perfect Sabbath experience.

ISBN # 1-881283-18-6. Ages 6-8. Softcover. $6.95

The Passover Passage

Susan Atlas

Rebecca Able is having a most memorable Passover. She is sailing in the Caribbean with her grandparents aboard their sailboat, the Diaspora. On this unforgettable trip, Becca learns not only how a Passover Seder is celebrated on board a sailboat, but also about freedom, opportunity, family, and Judaism. A real adventure.

ISBN #0-933873-46-8. Ages 8-11. Softcover. $5.95

New! The Saturday Secret

Miriam Rinn

Jason Siegel thinks his stepfather's new religious observances have gone far enough. First only kosher food at home. Then he is forced to wear a kippah (yarmulke). Now no baseball games on Shabbat! Jason is determined to play ball—no matter what. But his plan backfires and Jason finds himself entangled in a situation that hurts his teammate's feelings and jeopardizes his relationship with his mother and step-father.

ISBN #1-881283-26-7. Ages 8-12. Softcover. $6.95

Sing Time

Bruce Siegel

A ten-year-old "master of the fast comeback" discovers how a Cantor can impact his life. This Cantor doesn't just sing songs, he shares the value of a single moment in time, and teaches readers how music is the "calendar" of Jewish life. Cantor Jacobs steers our hero down a path he might never have taken otherwise.

ISBN #0-881283-14-3. Ages 8-12. Softcover $6.95

The Swastika on the Synagogue Door

J. Leonard Romm

When a suburban synagogue on Long Island is attacked by anti-Semitic vandals, the hatred manifest in the spray paint forces the Lazarus kids to confront their own history, their own prejudice, and find the guilty party.

ISBN #1-881283-05-4. Ages 10-14. Softcover. $6.95

Tanta Teva and the Magic Booth

Joel Lurie Grishaver

In this fantastic Sukkot novel, Marc meets Tanta Teva, a cleaning lady who is busy scrubbing graffiti off rocks in the forest. They proceed to travel in her Magic Sukkah to meet Biblical heroes in their childhood—Joshua, David and Hillel. On his journey Marc learns a lot about the history of the Sukkah and its modern values.

ISBN #1-881283-00-3. Ages 8-11. Softcover. $5.95

Two Cents and a Milk Bottle

Lee Chai'ah Batterman

This beautifully written juvenile novel affords students in both social studies and literature classrooms the opportunity to study an important period in American history from a distinctly Jewish perspective. Narrated by twelve-year-old Leely Dorman, the daughter of Russian immigrants living in Brooklyn, readers learn of the trials and tribulations of life during the Great Depression.

ISBN #1-881283-17-8. Ages 8-11. Hardcover. $15.95

Order books via
the Torah Aura Productions Website
at WWW.ALEFDESIGN.COM
or call Alef Design Group at
(800) 845-0662 or (323) 582-1200